Arrow to the Sun

a Pueblo
Indian tale
adapted and
illustrated

by Gerald McDermott

Troll Associates

PUFFIN BOOKS
Published by the Penguin Group
Viking Penguin Inc., 40 West 23rd Street, New York, New York 10010, U.S.A.
Penguin Books Ltd, 27 Wrights Lane, London W8 5TZ, England
Penguin Books Australia Ltd, Ringwood, Victoria, Australia
Penguin Books Canada Ltd, 2801 John Street, Markham, Ontario, Canada L3R 1B4
Penguin Books (N.Z.) Ltd, 182–190 Wairau Road, Auckland 10, New Zealand

Penguin Books Ltd, Registered Offices: Harmondsworth, Middlesex, England

First published by The Viking Press 1974
Published in Puffin Books 1977
10 9 8 7 6 5 4

Library of Congress Cataloging in Publication Data
McDermott, Gerald, Arrow to the sun.
SUMMARY: An adaptation of the Pueblo Indian myth which explains
how the spirit of the Lord of the Sun was brought to the world of men.
[1. Pueblo Indians—Legends]   I. Title.   PZ8.1.M159Ar
291.2 12 [398.2] [E] 76-53661
ISBN: 0 14 050.211 4
Story and Research Consultant: Charles Hofmann
Printed in the United States of America

Set in Clarendon Semibold

For Beverly, more than ever

Long ago the Lord of
the Sun sent the spark
of life to earth.

It traveled down the rays of the sun, through the heavens, and it came to the pueblo. There it entered the house of a young maiden.

In this way, the Boy came into the world of men.

He lived and grew and played in the
pueblo. But the other boys would not
let him join their games. "Where is
your father?" they asked. "You have no
father!" They mocked him and chased
him away. The Boy and his mother
were sad.

"Mother," he said one day, "I must look
for my father. No matter where he is, I
must find him."

So the Boy left home.

He traveled through the world of men
and came to Corn Planter. "Can you
lead me to my father?" he asked. Corn
Planter said nothing, but continued
to tend his crops.

The Boy went to Pot Maker. "Can you lead me to my father?" asked the Boy. Pot Maker said nothing, but continued to make her clay pots.

Then the Boy went to Arrow Maker, who was a wise man. "Can you lead me to my father?" Arrow Maker did not answer, but, because he was wise, he saw that the Boy had come from the Sun. So he created a special arrow.

The Boy became the arrow.

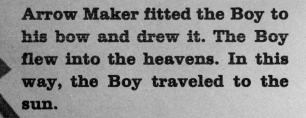

Arrow Maker fitted the Boy to his bow and drew it. The Boy flew into the heavens. In this way, the Boy traveled to the sun.

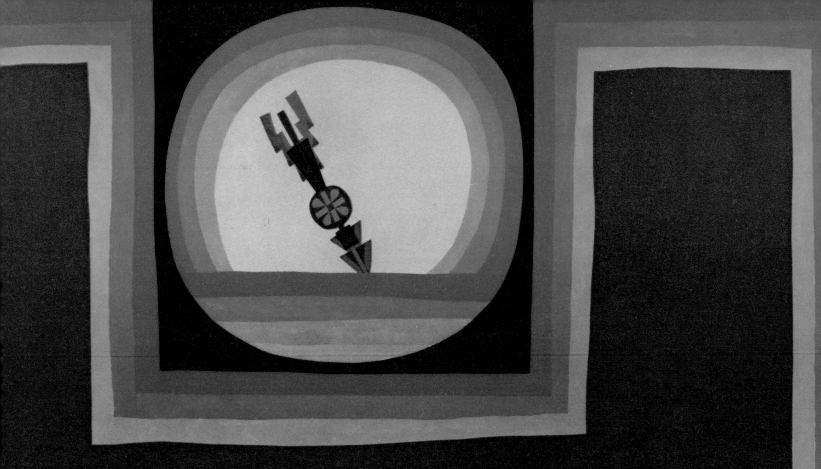

When the Boy saw the mighty Lord, he cried, "Father, it is I, your son!"

"Perhaps you are my son," the Lord replied, "perhaps you are not. You must prove yourself. You must pass through the four chambers of ceremony—the Kiva of Lions, the Kiva of Serpents, the Kiva of Bees, and the Kiva of Lightning."

The Boy was not afraid,
"Father," he said,
"I will endure these trials."

When the Boy came from the Kiva of Lightning, he was transformed. He was filled with the power of the sun.

The father and his son rejoiced.
"Now you must return to earth,
my son, and bring my spirit to
the world of men."

Once again the Boy became the arrow. When the arrow reached the earth, the Boy emerged and went to the pueblo.

The people celebrated his return in the
Dance of Life.

ABOUT THE ARTIST

GERALD MCDERMOTT began studying art at the Detroit Institute of Arts when he was four years old. He attended Pratt Institute in Brooklyn, where he received his bachelor's degree. With ARROW TO THE SUN Mr. McDermott is continuing a cycle of films and books that explores his special interest in folklore and mythology. He describes his latest work as "perhaps the most successful in terms of what I have wanted to achieve thus far." Mr. McDermott has made many films, and his unique style of film animation has brought him world-wide recognition.

Mr. McDermott is also the author-illustrator of THE STONECUTTER: A JAPANESE FOLK TALE.

ABOUT THE BOOK

The art work for this book was rendered in gouache and ink; the black line was preseparated. The art was reproduced in four-color process.